Buddy Bear and the Bad Guys

by
MARGERY CUYLER

Illustrated by
JANET STEVENS

CLARION BOOKS · **NEW YORK**

For Thomas,
my little good guy —*M.C.*

For Blake —*J.S.*

Clarion Books • a Houghton Mifflin Company imprint
215 Park Avenue South, New York, NY 10003 • Text copyright © 1993 by Margery Cuyler
Illustrations copyright © 1993 by Janet Stevens • All rights reserved.
For information about permission to reproduce selections from this book, write to Permissions,
Houghton Mifflin Company, 215 Park Avenue South, New York, NY 10003.
Printed in the U.S.A.

Library of Congress Cataloging-in-Publication Data • Cuyler, Margery.
  Buddy Bear and the bad guys / by Margery Cuyler ; illustrated by Janet Stevens. • p.   cm.
  Summary: Shy Buddy Bear is terrorized by three bullying raccoons until he decides to stand up to them.
  ISBN 0-395-59939-3 • [1. Bullies—Fiction.   2. Bears—Fiction.   3. Raccoons—Fiction.] • I. Stevens, Janet, ill. II. Title.
PZ7.C997Bar   1993   [E]—dc20   92-11576   CIP   AC
BVG   10 9 8 7 6 5 4 3 2 1

Buddy Bear lived with his mama and papa in the forest. One day, he decided to go berry picking. "I'll pick some berries for Mama and Papa, too," he thought.

He picked and picked until his pail was full. Just
as he was leaving, three Bad Guys dropped from a tree.
They grabbed the pail and ran into the forest.

"Help!" cried Buddy Bear. His heart beat like a drum.
His legs quivered like a hummingbird. He turned and
dashed all the way home.

"What's wrong?" asked Papa.

"Three Bad Guys stole my pail!" cried Buddy Bear.

"What did they look like?" asked Mama.

"Raccoons, I think," said Buddy Bear. "They were wearing bandanas and smelled like dead fish."

"Oh my," said Mama. "They do sound scary."

"Nonsense," said Papa. "Raccoons aren't scary. They just look that way. Don't forget, Buddy— bears are *bigger* than raccoons."

"Even little bears like me?"

"Even little bears like you," said Papa.

The next morning, Buddy Bear woke up hungry.

"I'm going fishing," he said.

"Bring home a fish for me," said Papa.

"And me," said Mama.

Buddy Bear sat by the water. He waited and waited for a
fish to come along. Finally, a fish swam by. Buddy Bear
struck it with his paw. Then he grabbed it and swallowed it.

Another fish came along and Buddy Bear
struck that one, too. "This one's for Papa,"
he said. But as he was picking it up, the three
Bad Guys jumped out from behind a bush.
"Give us that fish!" they yelled.

Buddy Bear's heart beat like a drum. His legs quivered
like a hummingbird. He dropped the fish and ran as fast as
he could all the way home.

"Where's my fish?" asked Papa.

"And mine?" asked Mama.

Buddy Bear hung his head. Then he began to cry. "The Bad Guys were hiding near the stream and they jumped out from behind a bush and told me to give them Papa's fish. I was so scared I dropped it."

Papa pulled Buddy Bear onto his lap. "I don't blame you for being frightened," he said. "But those Bad Guys can't hurt you. Remember what I told you? Bears are *bigger* than raccoons."

"I know," said Buddy Bear. "But I'm still scared."

"Don't worry," said Papa. "I'll go find those Bad Guys. And when I do, I'll frighten them so much they'll leave the forest forever!"

Papa Bear looked for the Bad Guys everywhere.

In hollow trees.

Next to streams.

By the berry patch.

But the Bad Guys weren't anywhere.

"Maybe they've left the forest," said Papa when he got home.
"Maybe they're just hiding," said Buddy Bear.

A few weeks later, Buddy Bear climbed a tree to
get a honeycomb. He was licking his sticky paws
when he heard a scratching noise. He looked down.
The Bad Guys were climbing up the trunk.

"Oh no!" cried Buddy Bear. "They're back!"

"Give us that honeycomb!" yelled the Bad Guys.

Buddy Bear was so scared he almost fell off the branch.
The Bad Guys jumped up beside him and grabbed the honey.

Buddy Bear's heart beat like a drum. His legs quivered like
a hummingbird. He tried to remember what his father had said.
I'll frighten them so much, they'll leave the forest forever.

Buddy Bear's fur bristled. His eyes blazed. "If Papa could scare them, so can I," he thought. "I'm going to get those Bad Guys, no matter what!"

Buddy Bear quietly shook the branch.
The Bad Guys wobbled back and forth.
"Give me back my honey," said Buddy Bear
in a small voice.
"No!" yelled the Bad Guys.

Buddy Bear felt braver. He shook the branch harder.
"Give me back my honey!" he said in a louder voice.
"Never!" shouted the Bad Guys.
Now Buddy Bear felt very brave. He shook the branch
so hard, the Bad Guys fell off.

They landed with a bump on the ground.

"Ouch!" they yelled. And they dropped the honeycomb.

Buddy Bear climbed quickly down the tree. He stood over the Bad Guys.

"Now get out of this forest," he growled.

"You can't make us," said the Bad Guys. Their voices were starting to quake.

"Oh yes I can," said Buddy Bear. "I can, because, because...I'm *bigger* than you!" And he really felt bigger.

He picked up the Bad Guys.
"Help!" they yelled.
He held them by their tails
and shook them.

"Stop!" they cried.

"Not unless you promise to leave," said Buddy Bear.

"We promise, we promise," they cried.

Buddy Bear let go. The Bad Guys landed in a heap.

"Let's get out of here!" the Bad Guys shouted.
"Bears are scary, even little bears."
  They turned and ran as fast as they could
out of the forest.

Buddy Bear picked up the honeycomb. Then he turned
and ran home as fast as he could to Mama and Papa.

He gave them the honey and told them about the Bad Guys.

"See how big and strong you are?" said Papa. "I bet those Bad Guys are gone for good."

"I bet so too," said Buddy Bear. "But if they come back, I'll know how to act. I'll act like a great big Papa Bear."

Buddy Bear climbed into Papa's lap. "But right now,
I like being a little bear."
He leaned against Papa's shoulder and fell asleep.